Big Cat

by Pipa Goodheart

Illustrated by Sandra Aguilar

Crabtree Publishing Company

www.crabtreebooks.com

Crabtree Publishing Company
www.crabtreebooks.com
1-800-387-7650

616 Welland Ave.
St. Catharines, ON
L2M 5V6

PMB 59051, 350 Fifth Ave.
59th Floor,
New York, NY

Published by Crabtree Publishing in 2011

Series Editor: Jackie Hamley
Editors: Melanie Palmer, Reagan Miller
Series Advisor: Catherine Glavina
Series Designer: Peter Scoulding
Project Coordinator: Kathy Middleton

Text © Pippa Goodhart 2010
Illustration © Sandra Aguilar 2010

Printed in Hong Kong/042011/BK20110304

First published in 2010
by Franklin Watts
(A division of Hachette
Children's Books)

The rights of the author and the
illustrator of this Work have been
asserted.

**Library and Archives Canada
Cataloguing in Publication**

Goodhart, Pippa
    Big Cat / by Pippa Goodhart ; illustrated by Sandra
Aguilar.

(Tadpoles)
ISBN 978-0-7787-0574-1 (bound).--
ISBN 978-0-7787-0585-7 (pbk.)

        I. Aguilar, Sandra II. Title. III. Series: Tadpoles
(St. Catharines, Ont.)

PZ10.3.G66Bi 2011   j823'.914   C2011-900149-7

**Library of Congress
Cataloging-in-Publication Data**

Goodhart, Pippa.
    Big Cat / by Pippa Goodhart ; illustrated by Sandra
Aguilar.
        p. cm. -- (Tadpoles)
    Summary: Big Cat likes to catch and play with mice,
but eventually the tables are turned.
    ISBN 978-0-7787-0585-7 (pbk. : alk. paper) --
ISBN 978-0-7787-0574-1 (reinforced library binding :
alk. paper)
    [1. Cats--Fiction. 2. Mice--Fiction.] I. Aguilar, Sandra,
ill. II. Title. III. Series.

    PZ7.G6125Big 2011
    [E]--dc22
                                        2010052359

Here is a list of the words in this story.
Common words:

a	not	the
and	now	then
big	said	with
is	that	

Other words:

cat	mice	six	together
fair	only	squeak	two
mouse	play	three	
meow	played		

Big Cat played ...

3

... with a mouse.

"Squeak! That is not fair!"

Big Cat played ...

... with two mice.
"Squeak, squeak!
That is not fair!"

9

Big Cat played ...

10

11

... with three mice.
"Squeak, squeak, squeak!
That is not fair!"

13

Then six mice ...

... played with
Big Cat.
"SQUEAK!"

16

"Meow!"
said Big Cat.

18

19

Now Big Cat and
the mice ...

... play together!

Puzzle Time

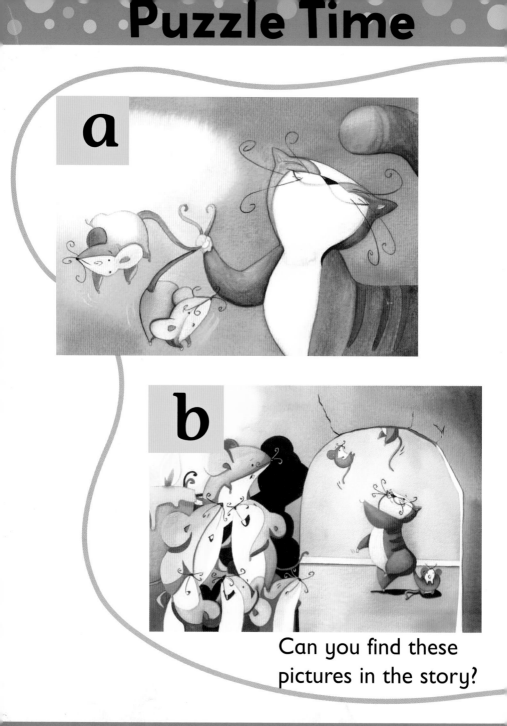

a

b

Can you find these
pictures in the story?

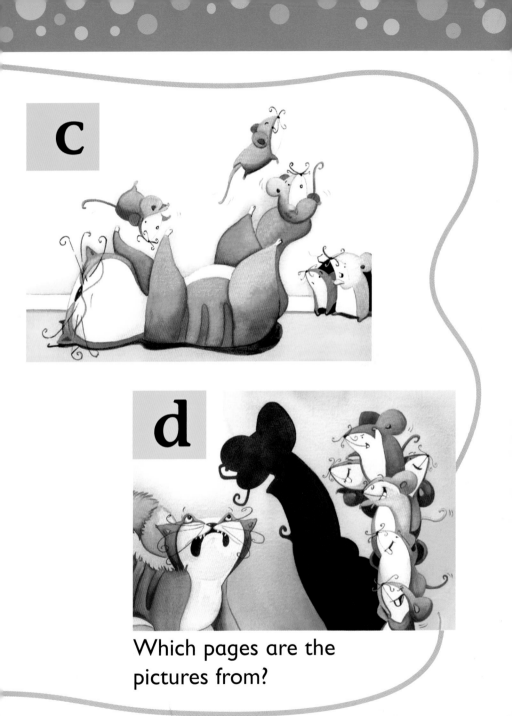

Which pages are the
pictures from?

Turn over for the answers!

Answers

The pictures come from these pages:
a. pages 8 and 9
b. pages 14 and 15
c. pages 12 and 13
d. pages 16 and 17

Notes for adults

Tadpoles are structured to provide support for early readers. The stories may also be used by adults for sharing with young children.

Starting to read alone can be daunting. **Tadpoles** help by listing the words in the book for a preview before reading. **Tadpoles** also provide strong visual support and repeat words and phrases. These books will both develop confidence and encourage reading and rereading for pleasure.

If you are reading this book with a child, here are a few suggestions:

1. Make reading fun! Choose a time to read when you and the child are relaxed and have time to share the story.

2. Look at the picture on the front cover and read the blurb on the back cover. What might the story be about? Why might the child like it?

3. Look at the list of words on page two. Can the child identify most of the words?

4. Encourage the child to retell the story using the jumbled picture puzzle on pages 22-23.

5. Discuss the story and see if the child can relate it to his or her own experiences, or perhaps compare it to another story he or she knows.

6. Give praise! Children learn best in a positive environment.

If you enjoyed this book, why not try another **TADPOLES** story?
Please see the back cover for more **TADPOLES** titles.
Visit **www.crabtreebooks.com** for other **Crabtree** books.